Dorothy
AND
TOTO

by Debbi Michiko Florence

Little Dog Lost

Dorothy AND TOTO

Little Dog Lost

by Debbi Michiko Florence

illustrated by Monika Roe

PICTURE WINDOW BOOKS

a capstone imprint

Wizard of Oz: Dorothy and Toto
is published by Picture Window Books,
a Capstone Imprint
1710 Roe Crest Drive
North Mankato, Minnesota 56003
www.mycapstone.com

CAPS34785

Library of Congress Cataloging-in-Publication Data
Names: Florence, Debbi Michiko, author.
Title: Dorothy and Toto. Little dog lost /
by Debbi Michiko Florence.
Other titles: Little dog lost
Description: North Mankato, Minnesota : Picture Window Books,
a Capstone imprint, [2016] | Series: Warner Brothers. Dorothy
and Toto | Summary: Dorothy and all her friends in the Land of
Oz help her find her lost
dog, Toto.
Identifiers: LCCN 2016011094| ISBN 9781479587056
(library binding) | ISBN 9781479587094 (paperback) | ISBN
9781479587131 (ebook (pdf))
Subjects: LCSH: Gale, Dorothy (Fictitious character)—Juvenile
fiction. | Toto (Fictitious character)—Juvenile fiction. | Oz
(Imaginary place)—Juvenile fiction. | Dogs—Juvenile fiction. |
Lost articles—Juvenile fiction. | CYAC: Dogs—Fiction. | Lost
and found possessions—Fiction. | Friendship—Fiction.
Classification: LCC PZ7.1.F593 Dm 2016 | DDC [E]—dc23
LC record available at http://lccn.loc.gov/2016011094

Designer: Alison Thiele
Editor: Jill Kalz
illustrated by Monika Roe

Printed in the United States of America.
009915R

Table of Contents

Chapter 1

Garden Trouble

Dorothy Gale and her dog, Toto, live in the Land of Oz.

Every morning Dorothy waters her garden. She tells the flowers her plans for the day.

One morning Dorothy said to Rose, "Today I am going to relax."

"What does that mean?" Rose asked.

"It means I will rest," Dorothy said.

"I will sit in the sun and read a book."

"A quiet day at home sounds nice," Daisy said.

"I will relax today too," said Fern.

But the quiet didn't last long.

BARK, BARK! BARK, BARK!

"Uh-oh. Toto, what's wrong?" Dorothy asked.

BARK, BARK! BARK, BARK!

Toto had spotted a squirrel in the garden. It was digging holes and making a mess. Toto knew the squirrel didn't belong in the garden. He chased after it.

The squirrel ran around Dorothy's legs. It knocked the watering can out of her hand. Water splashed everywhere.

"Oh, dear!" Dorothy cried.

Toto and the squirrel raced in circles. They made Dorothy dizzy.

The squirrel ran past Fern. Toto followed, barking loudly.

"Help! Help!" Fern shouted.

Finally the squirrel leapt over the gate and ran out of the garden. Toto did too.

"Toto, come back!" Dorothy called.

But Toto was gone.

Chapter 2

The Search Begins

"Oh, no!" Dorothy exclaimed.

"Little Toto is a hero," Rose said. "He saved us from the squirrel!"

"Toto!" Dorothy called.

"I'm sure he will come back, Dorothy," Daisy said.

Dorothy waited. But Toto did not return. Dorothy missed her dog.

"I must find Toto," Dorothy said. "I will relax another day."

She went into the house and got Toto's favorite squeaky toy. She also got his favorite treat. Toto loved bacon. Then Dorothy set out to find her dog.

As Dorothy walked she called out,
"Toto! Toto! Come home, Toto!"

Soon she met Milton the Munchkin
and his ducklings. "What's wrong,
Dorothy?" Milton asked.

"Toto ran after a squirrel, and I can't find him," Dorothy said.

"I will help you look for him," Milton said. "The ducklings will help too."

Dorothy took out Toto's favorite toy and squeezed it. **SQUEAK! SQUEAK!**

The ducklings quacked. **QUACK!**
QUACK! QUACK! QUACK!

"Toto always comes when I squeak
his toy," Dorothy explained.

The toy squeaked. The ducklings
quacked. But there was no sign of Toto.

"Let's go to Scarecrow's house," Milton said. "Maybe Toto is there."

"Good idea, Milton," Dorothy said. "Thank you!"

* * *

Scarecrow was standing in his yard. He waved.

"Scarecrow," Dorothy said, "have you seen Toto?"

"He ran past a little while ago," Scarecrow said, pointing. "He went that way, toward Tin Man's house."

"Let's hurry," Milton said. "Maybe we can catch him."

"I will help you," Scarecrow said. "Toto cannot have gone far."

Chapter 3

Don't Be Scared

Dorothy and her friends hurried down the Yellow Brick Road. They hoped they would find Toto before night came.

Dorothy knocked on Tin Man's door.

"Tin Man, have you seen Toto?" she said, trying not to cry.

"I'm sorry, Dorothy," Tin Man said.
"I was inside the house and did not see
Toto. But I will help you look for him."

Dorothy took out the strips of bacon. She waved them in the air. "Maybe if Toto smells his favorite treat, he will come back."

Everybody waited. But Toto did not come back. "Toto has never been lost before," Dorothy said. "What if he is very scared?"

"We will find him," Milton said. "Don't worry."

"Toto likes the woods," Dorothy said. "Let's look there."

Dorothy and her friends hurried to the woods. They called for Toto. Dorothy squeaked his toy and waved the bacon.

Still no sign of Toto.

"Look!" Milton pointed. "That bush is shaking!"

Dorothy ran to the bush. "Toto? Toto? Is that you?" she said.

The bush squeaked. A family of friendly weasels poked out their noses. No Toto.

Then something moved behind a tree.

"Is that Toto?" Scarecrow asked.

"No," Dorothy said, "that is the Cowardly Lion. Come out, Lion."

Two eyes peeked around the tree. "Oh, hello, friends," Lion said. "I was afraid of all the noise."

"Don't be scared. It is just us," Dorothy said. "Have you seen Toto?"

"No," Lion said, "but I can hear something. Listen."

Chapter 4

Old and New Friends

Dorothy and her friends stood still. They listened hard.

"Yes! I hear barking," Tin Man said.

"It sounds like Toto!" Scarecrow said.

"Oh, dear!" Dorothy cried. "What if Toto is in trouble?"

"I'm so scared!" Lion said.

Milton patted the Cowardly Lion to comfort him.

"The barking is coming from over there," Dorothy said. "I have never seen this path before."

"Me neither," Scarecrow said.

The friends peered down the path.

"I don't think we should go down there," Lion said, shaking. "We do not know where it goes."

"But I hear Toto," Dorothy said. "I must find him."

"We will go with you," Milton said.

All the friends bravely stepped onto the new path. As they walked the barking grew louder. The Cowardly Lion grabbed Tin Man's arm.

"Toto!" Dorothy called. "Toto, where are you?"

The path twisted and curved through the woods. The trees stood tall and close together. Dorothy could hear Toto, but she couldn't see him.

Then, suddenly, the path ended.

A pretty pink house sat at the end
of the path. In the yard were Toto and
a white dog with a pretty pink collar.
They were playing tag.

"Toto!" Dorothy cried.

Toto saw Dorothy and yipped loudly. He ran to her and jumped into her arms. Toto licked Dorothy's cheek.

"Toto, I was worried. I missed you very much!"

The door of the house opened. Out stepped a girl in a pretty pink dress. She wore a crown on her head.

"Hello!" she said. "My name is Glinda. This is my dog, Mini. Welcome to our home."

Dorothy and her friends smiled and introduced themselves.

"Mini's best friend moved away yesterday. She's been sad," Glinda said. "But Toto cheered her up today. He is a good new friend."

Dorothy smiled. "Toto and I are always happy to make new friends," she said.

"So are we," Glinda said. "Please join us for tea and cookies."

Everyone sat down and enjoyed the treats. They shared stories and laughed.

"I didn't read my book in the sun today," Dorothy said. "But this is a nice way to relax too. Spending time with old and new friends in the Land of Oz is great!"

About The Wizard of Oz

The Wizard of Oz follows young Dorothy Gale and her little dog, Toto, who are magically taken by tornado from Kansas to the Land of Oz. Dorothy sets off on the Yellow Brick Road and meets Scarecrow, Tin Man, and the Cowardly Lion. They join her on a dangerous journey to meet the Wizard of Oz, whose powers may help Dorothy return home.

The Wizard of Oz is one of the most beloved stories of all time. The book was written by L. Frank Baum and published in 1900. It was made into a movie starring Judy Garland in 1939.

Glossary

comfort (KUM-fert) — to make someone feel safe and at peace

cowardly (KOW-erd-lee) — not brave

duckling (DUCK-ling) — a young duck

favorite (FAY-ver-it) — liked best

introduce (in-troh-DOOS) — to tell someone your name when meeting for the first time

weasel (WEE-zel) — a long, thin furry animal with short legs

Use Your Brain

1. Why did Toto run away from home? Why didn't he come back right away?

2. Name Toto's two favorite things. Explain why Dorothy brought them along on the search for Toto.

3. Dorothy is a very kind person. Give examples of things she says or does that show her kindness.

About the Author

Debbi Michiko Florence writes books for kids and teens in The Word Nest, her writing studio that overlooks a pond. Her work includes two nonfiction books for kids and a chapter book series, Jasmine Toguchi. Debbi is a California native who currently lives in Connecticut with her husband, her little dog, and two ducks. She loves to travel around the world with her husband and daughter. Before she became an author, Debbi volunteered as a raptor rehabilitator and worked as an educator at a zoo.

About the Illustrator

Monika Roe was born with a passion for art. She grew up in a small town on California's central coast and couldn't wait to get to the big city, where she earned a degree in graphic design and entered the world of advertising. She worked as an award-winning art director and creative director in Los Angeles, California, and Indianapolis, Indiana, before becoming a full-time illustrator. Monika's studio is located in the redwood forest of California's Santa Cruz Mountains. There she creates illustrations for people throughout the world while her pug snores loudly in the background.

CHECK OUT MORE

Dorothy AND TOTO

ADVENTURES!

The Disappearing Picnic
by Debbi Michiko Florence

Little Dog Lost
by Debbi Michiko Florence

The Hunt For the Perfect Present
by Debbi Michiko Florence

What's Your Name?
by Debbi Michiko Florence